GARFIELD
STORIES

Including *The Big Star, Garfield's Picnic Adventure,
Garfield and the Space Cat*

Created by Jim Davis

Stories by Norma Simone, Jack C. Harris,
and Leslie McGuire
Illustrated by Mike Fentz

A GOLDEN BOOK • NEW YO
Western Publishing Company, Inc., Racine, W

D1578403

The Big Star

One sunny day Garfield sat in the window, looking at the world outside. He saw bees gathering nectar, birds building a nest, and squirrels chasing each other through the trees.

"It's a pretty day," Garfield thought. He yawned. "Pretty boring, that is.

"How can I beat this boredom?" Garfield asked himself. "I know! I'll tie Odie's ears in a knot!"

So Garfield tied Odie's ears in a knot. But it wasn't much fun, because Odie was too dumb even to notice.

"Dumb dog, dumb day," said Garfield.

"Jon, I need some excitement in my life," said Garfield.

Jon Arbuckle looked up from his newspaper. "Listen to this, Garfield," he said. "Fussy Cat Brand Cat Food is looking for a cat to star in a TV commercial. They're holding auditions today."

"How terribly uninteresting," said Garfield.

"The cat they choose gets a year's supply of Fussy Cat Brand Cat Food," said Jon.

"I'd rather have lasagna," said Garfield.

"Plus a year-long, all-expense-paid trip around the world," said Jon.

"A trip around the world! That's the kind of excitement I need! Let's go!" Garfield said, dragging Jon toward the door.

Garfield and Jon went to the TV studio.

"We're here to audition for the Fussy Cat commercial," Jon told the secretary.

"Tell the Fussy Cat people that their new star has arrived," said Garfield.

"Get in line," said the secretary.

There must have been a hundred owners and their cats waiting to audition for the commercial. Garfield and Jon were at the end of the line.

"A star like me should not have to wait," said Garfield.

So Garfield thought of a great trick.

He leaned over to the cat next to him.

"Say, did you hear about that accident over on Main Street?" said Garfield loudly. "A truck full of fresh fish and a truck full of cream both flipped over. Main Street is one gigantic lunch!"

With that, at least fifty cats leapt from their owners' arms and raced out the door toward Main Street. The surprised owners raced after them.

"What's going on?" said Jon.

"Guess they were afraid to face the camera," said Garfield with a smile.

An assistant director asked Jon some questions. "Does your cat have any special talents?" he asked.

"Just eating and sleeping," said Jon. "Oh, and he does a great imitation of an orange beach ball," he added, laughing.

"Remind me to shred your favorite chair when we get home," Garfield said to Jon.

Finally there was just one more cat ahead of Garfield. Garfield watched him audition. In front of the camera was a bowl of Fussy Cat Brand Cat Food. Beside the bowl was a big bag filled with more Fussy Cat Brand Cat Food. The cat walked up to the bowl, smiled at the camera, and began to eat neat little mouthfuls.

Garfield jumped from Jon's arms and raced onto the stage. "This commercial isn't big enough for both of us," said Garfield, bumping the other cat aside.

Garfield flashed the director a big smile. "You want a cat who can eat?" Garfield asked. "I'll show you a cat who can eat!"

Garfield picked up the bowl of Fussy Cat Brand Cat
Food, flipped the food into his mouth, and swallowed it
in one gulp!

"Amazing!" said the director.

But Garfield didn't stop there. He ripped open the big bag of Fussy Cat Brand Cat Food and began pouring the food into his mouth. In an instant he had finished the entire bag.

"Incredible!" shouted the director. "We've found our Fussy Cat!"

"Burp," said Garfield.

The director planned to shoot the commercial that
very afternoon. There was a lot of preparation to do. First
he brought in a hairdresser for Garfield.

"Just trim a little off the tummy," said Garfield.

At the same time a manicurist filed and polished
Garfield's claws.

Then the wardrobe people brushed Garfield's fur until it was smooth and shiny. Garfield purred happily.

"This is the life," thought Garfield. "The bright lights, the cameras, the excitement—I was born to be a star!"

"This is great, Garfield," said Jon. "Thanks to you, we'll soon be off on a year-long trip around the world!"

"Oh, I'm sorry, Mr. Arbuckle," said the director. "Only Garfield will be going on our world tour. But we do have a nice Fussy Cat Brand Cat Food calendar for you."

"Gee, thanks," said Jon sadly.

"I'll send you a postcard," said Garfield.

Now Garfield was having second thoughts about his new, exciting life. He hadn't counted on being apart from Jon and Odie for a whole year. He thought of all the dumb things Odie would do in a year, and all the dumb things Jon would say. Garfield would miss all that.

"It's tough being a star," said Garfield. "Fortunately, I'm big enough to handle it."

It was time to start filming.

"Here's all your cat has to do," the director said to
Jon. "He goes to the bowl marked 'Brand X,' sniffs it, and
walks away. He does the same thing with the bowl marked
'Brand Y.' But when he comes to the bowl marked 'Fussy
Cat,' he gobbles it down. Any questions?"

"When do I get my nap break?" said Garfield with a
yawn.

"Places, everybody," said the director. "And…
ACTION!"

Garfield walked up to the "Brand X" cat food. He
sniffed it and walked away.

"Good, good," said the director.

Then Garfield sniffed the "Brand Y" cat food and
walked away.

"Excellent, excellent," said the director.

Finally Garfield came to the Fussy Cat Brand Cat Food. He sniffed it carefully. He leaned closer to the bowl. He opened his mouth.

"That's it. That's it," said the director.

Suddenly Garfield felt *very* full and *very* sleepy. "I think I overdid my audition," he said. And with that he fell fast asleep—facedown—in the food!

"CUT! CUT!" yelled the director.

That night Jon fixed Garfield a special lasagna dinner. "You know, Garfield," said Jon, "I'm glad you didn't make that commercial. Odie and I would have missed you."

"BARK!" said Odie in agreement.

"I guess the part wasn't right for me," said Garfield. But he didn't really mind not being the star of a commercial. "However," he said, "I'll always be the biggest star in this house!"

Garfield's
Picnic Adventure

"I smell food," thought Garfield as he woke up from a sound sleep. He jumped up and ran to the kitchen as fast as his fat little legs could carry him.

Odie was already there. So was Jon, who said, "It's a beautiful day, so I'm packing a picnic lunch we can enjoy in the great outdoors."

"Oh, no," Garfield said to himself. "That means waiting an hour in a hot car before I get to dig into the picnic goodies."

"Whoops," said Jon. "I forgot pickles. I'll go out and buy some, but I'd better make sure you two don't sneak any food while I'm gone."

Jon tied the picnic basket shut with a string. "That ought to keep Garfield out," he said.

"Whoop-de-do," thought Garfield. "That itty-bitty string won't stop me. With some guidance from me, Odie will chew right through it."

Jon tied a rope to Odie's collar and attached the other end to a doorknob. "We can't have you helping Garfield break into the basket, can we?" he said as he left.

"I've lived here too long," Garfield complained. "Jon knows what I'm planning before I even think of it."

Garfield crept over to Odie and whispered in his ear. "Do you know what's in the basket, Odie, old pal? Hot dogs, potato salad, pretzels..."

The more Garfield talked about food, the more Odie's mouth watered. Soon he began to chew, imagining the taste of the picnic goodies. Garfield quickly stuck the rope between Odie's teeth. After a few loud chomps, Odie bit through it.

"You're free," Garfield cried happily, and the two pets raced toward the picnic basket.

"Now, Odie, take a bite out of this string, just like you did with the rope," Garfield instructed.

"Bark," Odie said, and he chewed the string until it broke. The picnic basket was open!

In an instant Garfield was gobbling down food. "This is the life," he said.

"Bark," said Odie, his mouth watering.

"Oh, yeah," said Garfield between bites. "Here's something for your help." He tossed Odie a half-eaten hot dog.

"Bark," said Odie, happy to get whatever he could.

It wasn't long before Jon returned. He was surprised
to find Odie greeting him at the door.

"Hey, wait a minute," Jon said as he walked into the
kitchen. "I left you tied up." Just then Jon noticed the
closed picnic basket and the broken string.

"Did I see that basket move?" Jon asked Odie.

"Bark, bark," Odie answered.

Jon flung open the basket lid only to find a stuffed Garfield smiling inside.

"Hello, Jon," he said. "What's for dessert?"

"Garfield!" Jon yelled. "You've spoiled the picnic for everyone. That food was supposed to be for me and Odie, too!"

"Bark!" said Odie.

Jon grabbed the basket as Garfield jumped to the floor.

"I'm still determined to go on our picnic. I'll pack a new lunch, but there will be no food for fat cats like you, Garfield. You can watch us eat."

"Oh, no," moaned Garfield. "There's nothing I hate more than watching others eat when I can't."

After an hour's ride in a hot car, they arrived at the park. Garfield took one look at all the kids playing ball and flying kites and he grew very excited.

"I'll bet there are plenty of kids who would feed a poor hungry kitty like me. All I have to do is act cute."

Purring loudly, Garfield snuggled up to a sad-looking little girl.

"Oh, what a pretty orange kitty," she said. "You're so friendly, you make me forget that my kite got lost in the trees. My name is Jessie. Would you like to share my lunch?"

"It worked," thought Garfield joyfully.

Garfield was about to bite into her sandwich when Jon pulled him away.

"I'm sorry," Jon said, "this fat cat is being punished. Why don't you join me, Odie, and Garfield in a game of catch before eating?"

"Get serious," thought Garfield. "If you think I'm going to run after a stupid ball on an empty stomach, you've got another think coming." Then Garfield stalked into the woods to be by himself.

Hours passed as Garfield walked deeper and deeper into the woods, feeling sorry for himself. "Uh-oh," he thought as he looked around, "things are getting mighty dark around here. I think I'm lost!"

Garfield didn't know which way to go. All around him he saw the glowing eyes of the forest animals. "I love food," he thought, "but I don't want to BE food for anyone else!"

For a long time Garfield ran this way and that way through the woods, becoming more and more frightened. All around him the eerie eyes glowed in the dark. Suddenly he came face-to-face with the biggest pair of eyes of all!

"Arrrrgh!" screamed Garfield.

"Bark!" said a familiar voice.

Just then clouds moved away from a full moon high above, and the forest was not as dark as before.

"Odie!" cried Garfield. "Boy, I'm even glad to see you. You came looking for me, didn't you, old pal? Hey! Dogs are great hunters. You can lead us out of these dark woods. Let's go, boy!"

After what seemed like hours, Garfield looked down at the ground and saw animal tracks.

"Wait a minute," he said. "These tracks are OUR tracks. You've been leading us around in circles. I've heard you can't teach an old dog new tricks, but with Odie, you can't teach a stupid dog any tricks. We're still lost."

Just then Garfield heard a strange sound. "It sounds like crying," he whispered. "I'm too scared to cry, Odie, and you're too dumb to be scared. There must be someone else in these woods."

Quietly the two crept closer to the crying sound.

As the clouds moved away from the moon, Garfield saw that it was little Jessie.

"It's Jessie," he shouted. "She found us! We're saved."

Jessie said, "When Jon said he couldn't find you, Odie went to look for you. So did I. I followed Odie, and then I got lost."

"Just great," Garfield muttered. "If it keeps going like this, everyone will be lost in the woods with us."

Suddenly Garfield looked up and saw something high in a tree. The moonlight made it very clear.

"Look, it's Jessie's lost kite," he said. "If we follow the string, it will lead us back to the park."

They followed the string as it wound through the
trees and bushes. Soon they came to the edge of the
woods.

"There are the picnic grounds," Jessie shouted
happily.

"Bark, bark," said Odie.

There was a big crowd of people waiting at the edge
of the woods. Jon was there, too, with Jessie's parents.

Everyone celebrated around a campfire with another big picnic meal. Jon had forgotten all about being mad at Garfield.

"You guys are great," he said. "You're heroes. Everybody thinks you're wonderful."

"They're absolutely right," Garfield thought in between bites of a hot dog.

Odie couldn't think at all. His mouth was just too full.

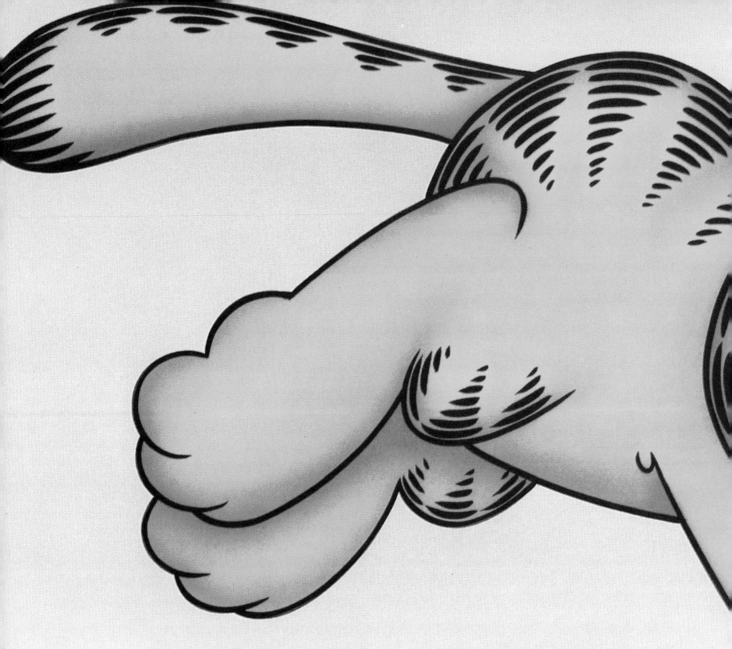

Garfield and the Space Cat

Garfield was enjoying his fifteenth nap of the afternoon when his favorite smell in the whole world floated past his nose. In a flash he was up and racing to the kitchen. Sitting unguarded on the counter was a freshly baked pan of lasagna!

"Say your prayers, lasagna," warned Garfield. "You are about to be gobbled!"

Garfield pounced.

At the last second Jon snatched the pan away. Instead of lasagna, Garfield wound up with a mouthful of countertop.

"No, you don't, Garfield," said Jon. "I'm taking this lasagna to a dinner party."

"I'll get you for this," grumbled Garfield.

Jon tossed Garfield out of the house. "I can't trust you with this lasagna," said Jon. "But if you behave, I'll bring you the leftovers."

"I wouldn't eat your old lasagna if it was the last lasagna on Earth," replied Garfield. "Well, maybe I would."

Still hungry, Garfield decided to check the garbage cans in the alley behind the market. But all he found in the first few garbage cans was garbage.

So imagine Garfield's surprise when he lifted the last lid and came face-to-face with a cat who looked just like himself, but with two silver antennae sticking out of his head!

"Who are you?" said Garfield.

"I am Fieldgar from the planet Catalon," said the new cat in a crackling, beeping voice. "Who are you?"

"I'm Garfield from down the street," said Garfield. "Do you mean that you're from outer space?"

"Outer, outer space, actually," said Fieldgar.

"What's a space cat doing in a garbage can?" asked Garfield.

"Garbage can?" said Fieldgar. "This is my stratospace cruiser. It has four carillium engines and a top speed of 50,000 warps per hour."

"Well, it could use a new paint job," said Garfield. "Climb out of there and I'll show you around my planet."

Fieldgar looked around cautiously. "All right," he said, "but we'll have to keep an eye out for the Cosmutts. They've been chasing me across the entire universe."

"We'll be careful," said Garfield, though he didn't know what Fieldgar was talking about.

Fieldgar stopped at the end of the alley. "What are those funny-looking creatures?" he asked.

"Those are people," said Garfield. "They think they run this planet, but we cats are actually in charge."

"We don't have people on Catalon," said Fieldgar.

"Sounds like a great place to me," thought Garfield.

"This is my vet's office," said Garfield. "A vet is an animal doctor. Watch out for people with needles."

"We don't need doctors on Catalon," said Fieldgar. "We cure everything with food."

Garfield really liked the sound of that!

Garfield took Fieldgar home to meet Odie. But when Odie came bounding out of the house, Fieldgar gasped in terror!

"It's an evil Cosmutt!" cried Fieldgar. "Run!"

Garfield grabbed Fieldgar. "That's not an evil Cosmutt," he said. "That's a dumb dog named Odie."

"He looks just like a Cosmutt," said Fieldgar in a shaky voice.

"Too bad for the Cosmutts," said Garfield.

When Odie saw two cats like Garfield, he was even more confused than usual. Finally he decided to give both of them a big, wet lick.

"Yech!" said Fieldgar. "He may not be evil, but he sure is sloppy."

Fieldgar decided that he had better blast back into space before the real Cosmutts tracked him down. He and Garfield were walking back to the garbage can cruiser when suddenly a spaceship shaped like a giant dog dish zoomed out of the sky right toward them!

"Cosmutts!" cried Fieldgar, diving behind a tree.

The spaceship landed in a cloud of smoke and dust. Out jumped the Cosmutts, who did indeed look just like Odie. They headed straight for Garfield!

"They think you're me!" Fieldgar shouted. "Take cover!"

"I can handle these dopey dogs," said Garfield.

"But they'll shoot you with their pasta blaster!" said Fieldgar.

"What's that?" asked Garfield.

Before Fieldgar could explain, one of the Cosmutts blasted Garfield with something that looked and smelled like warm tomato sauce, cheese, and noodles.

"Poor Garfield!" cried Fieldgar.

"Hey!" said Garfield, licking the messy stuff from his lips. "This tastes just like lasagna! In fact, it *is* lasagna!

"Blast me again!" Garfield shouted to the surprised Cosmutts. "Come on, give it your best shot! Make my day!"

The Cosmutts had never met a cat who could stand
up to their pasta blaster. They all yelped as they
scrambled back into their spaceship and zoomed away!
"Come back!" cried Garfield. "I'm still hungry!"

"You didn't get hurt!" said Fieldgar happily.

"On the contrary, I think I gained a few pounds," said Garfield, patting his tummy.

"Thanks for saving me," Fieldgar said. "That was very brave of you."

"I can lick any lasagna in the universe," said Garfield proudly.

When they got back to Fieldgar's spaceship, it was
filled with trash. "Why would anyone put this junk in my
cruiser?" asked Fieldgar, frowning. Garfield tried not to
laugh!

Finally the spaceship was ready to go.

"I'm going to send you a medal for bravery,"
promised Fieldgar.

"I'd prefer a pasta blaster," said Garfield.

With a wave and a roar Fieldgar blasted into space.

"You know, I'm really going to miss him," thought Garfield sadly. "But not as much as I'm going to miss those Cosmutts!"

Then Garfield had a happy thought. "Hey, I wonder if Jon saved me any of that lasagna he made…"